The Robbers

by
Josh Lacey

Illustrated by Stephen Elford

You do not need to read this page – just get on with the book!

First published in 2009 in Great Britain by
Barrington Stoke Ltd
18 Walker St, Edinburgh, EH3 7LP

www.barringtonstoke.co.uk

ISBN: 978-1-84299-639-3

Printed in Great Britain by Bell & Bain Ltd

AUTHOR ID

Name: Josh Lacey

Likes: Reading *Tintin*, climbing up mountains and eating spaghetti.

Dislikes: Going shopping and being told what to do.

3 words that best describe me:
Joshua Thomas Lacey.

A secret not many people know:
I can juggle.

ILLUSTRATOR ID

Name: Stephen Elford

Likes: Good movies, bass guitar and taking things apart.

Dislikes: Rude people, reality TV and eating rhubarb.

3 words that best describe me:
Friendly, geeky, hairy.

A secret not many people know:
Spiders scare me. Even little ones.

Contents

Chapter 1
A Bag of Money

My friend Peter has a ten pound note pinned to his bedroom wall.

Do you want to know how it got there?

I'll tell you.

One Saturday morning, Peter walked into the bank. He was carrying a heavy plastic bag.

He joined the line.

The bank was often full on Saturday mornings, but it wasn't very full on that Saturday. There were three bank-clerks working behind the desk and only six people in front of Peter in the queue.

He had left his mum outside.

She was going to collect some pills from the chemist, and then buy some sausages from the butcher. Peter would go and find her as soon as he had put his money into his savings account.

He thought it would take about five minutes.

But he was wrong.

Chapter 2
The Woman with Green Eyes

The line moved fast. Peter was soon standing at the front.

The woman behind the desk said, "Next, please."

Peter walked forward and placed his plastic bag on the desk. He looked through the glass screen at the woman and said, "I want to pay this in, please."

She was a small woman with black hair and green eyes. She looked at the bag and gave a sigh. She knew Peter. He came here every Saturday. She also knew what would be inside the bag. She said, "How much is it today?"

"Thirty-eight pounds and ninety-four pence," said Peter.

"All in coins?"

"There's a ten pound note," said Peter. "But the rest is coins."

The clerk sighed again. "Go on, then. Pass it over."

Peter passed his bag under the glass screen. The woman took the bag and tipped it out onto her desk. Coins spilled in every direction. A few skidded across the desk, but she grabbed them before they could get away. She shook out the bag, checking that

4

there weren't coins stuck inside, then asked Peter if he wanted it back again.

"No, thanks," said Peter. "We've got lots of bags at home."

"I'm sure you have," said the woman. She sighed a third time and started sorting the coins into stacks.

Peter watched her carefully. He didn't want his money to go missing. Before Peter left home, he had counted it, so he would know if the clerk made a mistake.

He already knew how much he had in his account. He knew how close he was to his target. If he worked for another six or seven weekends, he should have enough. And then, at last, he would be able to buy what he wanted.

His own computer.

Peter had been saving for months. He did odd jobs at the weekends. He never spent any of his pocket money. He even walked to and from school with his eyes fixed on the pavement, hunting for coins.

It's amazing how many people drop money in the street. Next time you go out, you should have a look. You might get rich.

Peter found a coin almost every day. Normally just pennies. Sometimes silver fives or tens or twenties. Once or twice a month, he found a pound coin. And last week, walking home from school, he had found a ten pound note.

He had been staring at the pavement, hunting for coins, when he glimpsed something from the corner of his eye. He looked up. There was a piece of paper stuck in a bush, fluttering in the breeze. He knew at once what it was. He looked around. No one else was close. He darted forwards, grabbed the note and stuffed it in his pocket.

Peter didn't tell anyone what he'd found. He knew his mum and dad would try to talk him into taking it to the police station, but he wasn't going to do that. No way. This was his.

"Finders, keepers" was Peter's motto. If someone was stupid enough to drop ten pounds, then they shouldn't make a fuss about it.

Chapter 3
The Man in the Black Mask

The woman had counted about half of Peter's coins when there was a loud shout, "This is a hold-up! Put your hands in the air!"

The woman looked up. Her mouth dropped open.

Peter turned round.

There were three people standing in the middle of the bank. Their faces were covered with black masks.

The tallest man was carrying a sawn-off shot-gun. The others were holding pistols.

If you were walking down the street and you saw three people carrying guns and wearing black masks, you might giggle. *They're in fancy dress*, you'd say to yourself. *They must be going to a party*. But there was nothing funny about these three men. With their masks and their guns, they looked terrifying.

The tallest man lifted his shot-gun and pointed it at Peter. He spoke with a loud, deep voice.

"Don't do anything stupid," he said. "Or I will shoot this boy."

People turned their heads to look at Peter.

Peter didn't like people staring at him, but this was different. He didn't even notice them. All he could think about was the shot-gun. He stood very still and hoped he wasn't going to get shot.

"I will kill him," said the man in the mask. "If I have to." He turned his head from side to side, looking at every person in the room. He could see their faces even if they couldn't see his.

No one moved. No one spoke. But everyone understood what he meant.

The robber turned to look at Peter. He said, "Put your hands in the air."

Peter raised his hands very slowly into the air.

The robber said, "What's your name?"

"Peter."

"Don't do anything stupid, Peter," said the robber. He had a mean voice. "Don't move. Don't shout. Just stay where you are. OK?"

"OK," said Peter.

"Peter is going to stay just where he is," said the robber, talking to everyone in the bank. "But I want the rest of you to get down on the floor." He waved his shot-gun around the room. "Go on! Lie down! Right now!"

There were seven other people in the bank and three bank-clerks working behind the glass screen. None of them tried to argue. No one shouted or screamed or tried to grab one of the guns. They just did as they were told and lay on the floor.

The robber marched across the bank and stood beside Peter. He lifted his shot-gun and placed its tip against Peter's head.

Peter could feel the metal touching his skin. It was cold. He wanted to jump backwards or turn round and run away. More than anything, he wanted to get out of the bank. But he knew he mustn't move. He knew he just had to stand very, very still and do whatever he was told.

The robber looked through the glass screen at the woman with green eyes. He said, "Do you want this boy to die?"

"No," whispered the woman. She was so scared she could hardly speak.

"Then you must do just what I say," said the robber. "Do you understand?"

"Yes," whispered the woman.

"Speak louder! I can't hear you. Say it again. Do you understand?"

"Yes," whispered the woman. She cleared her throat and spoke a little louder. "Yes, I understand."

"Good," said the robber. "Now, I want you to open this door."

He pointed at the locked door that led to the back of the bank.

Chapter 4
The Panic Button

When the woman started working at the bank, she was given strict instructions by the manager. He told her what to do if there was a robbery.

Press the panic button, the manager said. *Wait for the police to arrive. But don't open the door to the back of the bank. Don't let them inside.*

The woman knew what would happen if she opened the door. She would lose her job. But she also knew what would happen if she didn't open the door. The robber would kill the boy.

Her green eyes darted from the robber's mask to Peter's face. She looked at the shot-gun. She felt sick with fear and panic.

Her face was white. Her hands were shaking. She was terrified.

And then the robber shouted at her again.

"Open the door!" he yelled. His voice sounded angry. "You'd better do it right now! Or this boy will die!"

He jabbed his shot-gun into Peter's head.

"Ow," said Peter.

He didn't mean to make a noise. But wouldn't you if someone hit your head with a shot-gun?

The woman stood up. Her mind had been made up. She didn't want to see Peter getting hurt. She pressed a button on the wall. The door opened.

"Thank you," said the robber. He pushed Peter towards the door. "Go on. You first."

Peter didn't understand what was happening. Why should he go through the door? Did the robber need his help? Was he going to be shot? But Peter knew that you shouldn't ask questions of men with guns. It's better just to do what they say. Peter stepped forwards, moving very slowly and carefully, not giving the robber any reason to shoot him, and went through the door.

Chapter 5
Money, Money, Money

The robber reached into his pocket and pulled out three black bin bags. He threw them to the woman. She caught them and stared at him with her green eyes.

"Pass them round," said the robber. "Fill them up. No coins, just notes. Do you understand?"

"I'll do whatever you want," said the woman. "But please don't hurt the boy."

"Stop talking so much!" said the robber. "Just fill up the bags. Go on! Fill 'em up!"

The woman passed two bags to the other two bank-clerks. They pulled out drawers in their desks, opened the bags and filled them with money.

Peter watched with wide eyes.

He saw bundles of five and ten and twenty pound notes. Coming out of the drawers. Dropping into the bags.

Each bundle of notes looked like a brick. Each was tied with a yellow strap. And any one of them would have been more than enough to buy the new computer that Peter wanted. He could buy five computers with one of those bundles. And have change for a printer.

He had been saving for months and he still didn't have enough for his computer.

These three men just walked into the bank, wearing masks and carrying guns, and took whatever they wanted.

It was so unfair.

Peter thought about his own money. Thirty-eight pounds and ninety-four pence. Mostly in coins. Plus one ten pound note. Sitting on the desk, waiting to be counted. If the robbery hadn't happened, that money would be in his savings account by now.

He could see the pile of his coins sitting on the desk. His ten pound note was perched on the top.

The woman didn't touch the coins or the note. The robber wasn't interested in coins or a grubby old ten pound note. He had more important things to worry about. Why steal a few coins when you can have thousands and thousands and thousands of pounds in crisp new notes?

It was done quickly. The bags were full. They looked like Father Christmas's sacks, stuffed with presents.

The woman looked at the robber and said, "What now?"

"You haven't finished," the robber said with a snarl. He pointed. "What about that?"

"What about what?" said the woman.

"That," said the robber, pointing at a ten pound note on the desk. "I want that too."

Peter couldn't believe it.

That was his ten pound note!

"You can have whatever you want," said the woman. "Just don't hurt anyone." She plucked the ten pound note from her desk and stuffed it into one of the bags. "Now you've got it. What else do you want?"

"I want you to bring those bags here," said the robber.

"Then I will," said the clerk. She collected the two bags from the other bank-clerks and took all three to the robber.

"Put them down there," said the robber. "On the floor."

The woman did as he said and put the three bags on the floor. She straightened up and looked at him, waiting for his instructions.

"You," said the robber, pointing at Peter. "Pick them up."

Peter blinked. "Me?"

"Go on, pick them up."

Peter picked up the three bags.

He had never thought that money could be so heavy.

"Now, get moving," said the robber. "Come on! Let's go!"

He pushed Peter towards the door.

Chapter 6
Thank You

Peter felt furious. He didn't care about the robbers. Nor did he care about the thousands and thousands and thousands of pounds that had been stuffed into these three bags. It belonged to the bank and the bank had lots of money. But he was intensely angry about his own ten pound note. It belonged to him. And he wanted it back.

He also wanted to tell the robber to get lost.

"Carry your own bags," he wanted to say. "Why should I carry them for you?"

Of course, he didn't say that. If a man points a shot-gun at you, you do whatever he tells you. You might not like it. You might not want to. But he's the one with the shot-gun, so you'd better do whatever he wants. Otherwise he might blow your head off.

Peter didn't want to lose his head. So he dragged the three heavy bags along the floor. The robber walked behind him, pointing the shot-gun at his back.

They walked back into the main part of the bank.

Nothing had changed. One of the masked men was standing at the door and the other was in the middle of the room. Both of them were pointing their pistols at the people on the floor, making sure that no one tried to be a hero.

The man with the shot-gun spoke loudly so everyone could hear him. "Thank you very much," he said. "You've all been very helpful. And very sensible. Please don't stop now. Stay where you are for a few more minutes and you won't get hurt. Someone will have called the police. They will be here soon. This will soon be over. Stay cool, stay calm and stay on the floor."

The robber turned to Peter and said, "Put the bags down. Right there."

Peter did as he was told.

"Thank you," said the robber. "Now, lie down."

"Why?" said Peter.

"Don't worry, you're going to be OK. No one is going to hurt you. Do as you're told and lie on the floor."

Peter didn't want to lie down. He wanted to reach into one of the bags and grab his ten pound note. But he knew he couldn't. He lay on the floor.

It was cold and uncomfortable. But he didn't move or complain.

He kept his eyes open. He stared at the floor. He waited.

He didn't understand what was going on. The robbers had the money. They knew the police were coming. Why didn't they run away now?

He felt a hand on his back.

The robber was leaning over him.

Peter felt terrified. What was happening? What did he want now?

The robber put his mouth close to Peter's ear and whispered, "Thanks for all your help, Peter. I couldn't have done it without you."

That was all he said. Then he patted Peter on the back, straightened up and walked away.

Chapter 7
The Green Car

Peter wanted to roll over and shout at the robber: "I don't want your thanks! I didn't want to help you! I only did it because you were pointing a shot-gun in my face!"

But he didn't move or speak.

He hoped the robber was right and one of the bank-clerks really had pressed a panic button. He didn't want to lie on the floor for too long.

Peter heard footsteps. The robbers were leaving the bank.

Taking three sacks of money. And Peter's ten pound note.

Peter remembered what the robber had said.

Thanks for all your help, Peter. I couldn't have done it without you.

Peter thought: Was that true? Had he really helped the robbers?

Peter lifted his head from the floor. He turned very slowly and stared at the door.

He could see the three robbers walking out of the bank. Each of them was holding a gun in one hand and a black bag in the other.

Peter looked around. No one else had moved. Everyone was lying on the floor, face-down, keeping quiet. They weren't going to move until the police arrived.

The last robber walked out of the bank. The door swung shut behind him. They were gone. They had got what they wanted and no one had been harmed.

Peter jumped to his feet and ran after them.

He didn't wonder what might happen to him. He didn't worry whether he was doing the right thing. In fact, he wasn't thinking at all. He just felt a rush of anger that three men could walk into a bank and walk out again with his ten pound note. He sprinted across the bank and sprang out of the door.

He looked both ways, searching the street for the robbers.

There they were!

A green car was parked in the street. The doors were open. The engine was running. A man was sitting in the front seat. He must have been the fourth member of the gang.

The three robbers threw their bags into the car, then jumped in and slammed the doors.

Peter ran after them.

The car pulled out. The driver could have sped down the street with a screech of tyres, but everyone would have turned to look at him. Instead, he drove slowly, trying to look normal.

Peter could see through the back window of the car. The three robbers had already removed their masks.

If you happened to walk down the street at that moment, you wouldn't have noticed anything strange. If you'd looked through the

windows of the green car, you would just have seen four ordinary men. They didn't look like criminals. You never would have guessed that they had just robbed a bank.

Peter knew what would happen next. The four men would drive away. They would vanish into the city. No one would ever find them. They would get away with three bags of money. And his ten pound note.

Peter wasn't going to let that happen.

He sprinted after the green car.

Chapter 8
The Chase

Peter ran down the street, weaving through shoppers. He jumped over a dog's lead. He dodged round an old lady. He banged into a fat man. He barged through a group of girls. He pushed past two boys.

He heard shouts behind him:

"Hey!"

"Watch where you're going!"

"That hurt!"

He wished he could stop and say sorry, but he didn't have time. The car had almost reached the end of the street.

He sped up.

A thought flashed through his mind. What would he do if he caught up with the car?

He knew he couldn't stop the robbers. They had guns and he had nothing. They would shoot him and drive away.

So what could he do?

Think about that later, he told himself. Catch them first. Then worry about what to do.

The car turned the corner. It was getting away from him. He'd have to run faster now. A lot faster.

He was already feeling tired. His legs hurt. But he forced himself to speed up.

He stared at the number plate and tried to remember the numbers and letters.

As he came closer to the corner, he noticed something.

Someone had left their bike outside a newsagent. They must have gone inside to buy a paper or some sweets and left their bike unlocked. Peter did that himself. If he was just leaving his bike for a few seconds, he didn't bother locking it. He was sure no one would steal it.

Big mistake.

Peter grabbed the bike. He swung himself onto the saddle, pushed his feet down on the pedals and rode away. He bumped off the pavement and sped up along the road.

He heard a shout behind him.

"That's my bike!"

Peter went faster.

He swept around the corner. Up ahead, he could see the green car. It had stopped at some traffic lights. They were turning from red to amber. The car pulled away and sped down the street.

Peter pushed on the pedals with all his strength.

He heard more shouts behind him. He turned his head and looked back.

Several people were running behind him. One was waving his arms. Another man was shouting. Others were using all their energy for running.

Peter knew what would happen when they caught him.

He focused on the road. The car was up ahead. He didn't want to lose it.

Now he could hear another noise too. The sound of police sirens. The police must have arrived at the bank. They would find seven people lying on the floor and three bank-clerks sheltering behind the glass screen, but no robbers. No money. And no sign of the boy who had been used by the robbers to get through the door.

They'll think I'm a robber too, thought Peter. *They'll accuse me of robbing the bank.*

Unless I catch the real robbers.

That was when he saw the two policemen.

They were walking along the street. The green car drove past them slowly, but they didn't turn their heads. They weren't interested in an ordinary car with four ordinary men inside. They were much more interested in a boy on a stolen bike being chased by an angry crowd.

The two policemen stepped into the road. One of them raised his arms. The other shouted, "Stop right there!"

Chapter 9
Enter the Chopper

Peter looked over his shoulder. He could see the people chasing him not far behind him. They were red-faced and furious.

The police on one side. An angry crowd on the other. And up ahead, getting further away with every second, the green car.

What should he do?

He could stop and explain everything. He could say sorry for stealing the bike and explain why he needed it. *I'm chasing bank robbers*, he could say. *And I'm not going to catch them on foot.* He could ask the police to call for back-up. He could suggest they stop the green car. He could tell them that each of the passengers would be holding a black bag on his lap – and each of the black bags would be stuffed to the brim with brand new five and ten and twenty pound notes.

By the time he said all that, the green car would be miles away.

He pushed down on the pedals with all his strength and soared towards the two policemen.

They held their arms out. Ready to stop him.

If he hit them, there would be a nasty crunch. Perhaps a broken leg or two. And the robbers would get away.

At the last moment, Peter yanked the handle-bars and turned them sharply to the left.

His tyres squealed on the tarmac.

He whistled past the police.

Just when he thought he was free, a hand grabbed his arm.

Peter was pulled sideways, and lost his balance. His hands lifted from the handle-bars. His feet slipped off the pedals. And he parted company with the bike. He went head over heels and landed in a heap with the policeman.

The bike shot down the road without a rider.

It hit the pavement and flipped over and smashed into a wall and rattled and banged and bent and twisted and came to a

shuddering stop in a heap of mangled metal and torn rubber.

Peter sat up and groaned.

His head hurt. His legs too. And his arms.

In fact, just about everything hurt.

But he didn't have time to think about that now. An angry crowd stood around him and two stern policemen. People were pushing forwards, pointing and shouting.

"He nicked her bike!" shouted one of them.

"It was him!" yelled a second. "I'd know him anywhere!"

"Look what he's done to that bike!" screeched a third.

A girl pushed forwards. She had long hair and glasses. "He stole my bike!" Tears dribbled down her face. "He's broken it too!"

Peter turned his head and looked at the bike. She was right. The crash had crushed it. Spokes had snapped. The wheels were bent. No one was going to be riding that bicycle for a long, long time.

Peter stood up slowly. People pushed forwards. Hands reached for him.

Peter saw a blur of open mouths and wild eyes. He felt scared. He wanted to run away. And then he remembered why he was here and what he had to do. He grabbed the sleeve of the nearest policeman and started telling him about the bank robbers. But not a word could be heard. His voice was lost under the noise of the angry crowd.

The police saw that he was trying to speak. One of them shouted, "Quiet! Quiet! Let's have a bit of respect, please!"

The crowd went silent. People murmured to one another, but no one shouted.

The two policemen turned to Peter.

One of them said, "What's your name?"

"You've got to stop the green car," said Peter.

"Just tell us your name," said the other policeman.

"My name doesn't matter," said Peter. "You've got to stop them! They've just robbed a bank."

He couldn't understand why, but his words seemed to make the crowd angry. People shouted and jeered. They weren't interested in green cars or bank robbers. All they wanted was justice for the girl whose bike had been stolen.

One of the policemen hushed the crowd and the other leaned down to speak to Peter. "What are you talking about? What have you seen?"

"Robbers," said Peter. "Someone's robbed … at the bank."

"I know," said the policemen. "We've just heard about it. But how do you know about it?"

"I was there," said Peter. "I was in the bank. I saw everything. I was chasing the robbers. If you hadn't stopped me, I would have caught them too."

The policeman stared into Peter's face, trying to make up his mind whether to believe him. He must have thought that Peter was telling the truth, because he had a few words with the other policeman, telling him to get rid of the crowd. And then he pulled Peter to one side and asked him some urgent questions.

Peter described the robbers and their green car. He pointed up the road, showing which way it had gone.

He said, "Do you want to know the number plate?"

"Can you remember it?" said the policeman.

"Of course I can," said Peter. And he could.

The policeman grabbed his radio and called for assistance.

Two minutes later, the sound of sirens filled the air.

A few moments after that, two police helicopters flew overhead, heading in the direction that the green car had taken.

Chapter 10
Finders Keepers

Peter didn't see the robbers being caught, but he heard about it afterwards. The police told him what happened. The two helicopters followed the green car and pin-pointed its position. More police came from every direction.

The robbers were trapped. They dumped the car and tried to run, but they didn't get far.

Not a shot was fired. The robbers had nowhere to go. They put down their guns and raised their hands in the air.

The police told Peter that he was both stupid and lucky. Stupid because you should never chase an armed man. Lucky that he didn't get shot.

But they also thanked him. They wouldn't have caught the robbers without his help.

The bank was grateful too. So grateful, in fact, that they paid Peter a large reward.

He had never had so much money.

He bought himself a new computer. He got a printer and a camera too. He tracked down the girl whose bike he had stolen and bought her a new one. And he put the rest of the money in the bank.

But not the ten pound note.

The bank gave it back to him.

He didn't spend it. Or put it in his savings account. He pinned it to his bedroom wall.

It's still there now.

Barrington Stoke would like to thank all its readers for commenting on the manuscript before publication and in particular:

Anna Begeer	Flora Leadley
Jonathan Brough	Laura de Lisle
Emilie Clarke	Mo Maynard
Priyanka Dutt	Mabel McCabe
Natalia Fishman	Lois Robinson
Isabel Fox	Simran Sohanpal
Eleanor Frame	Pink Squire
Martha Glynn	Isabelle Staunton
Tilly Holt	Kiran Uttamohandani
Tara Hughes	Isobel Voysey
Elyse Husain	Claudine Wallace
Anoushka Kohli	Áine Williams
Miranda Layton	Sophie Worsnop

Become a Consultant!

Would you like to give us feedback on our titles before they are published? Contact us at the email address below – we'd love to hear from you!

info@barringtonstoke.co.uk
www.barringtonstoke.co.uk

Great reads – no problem!

Barrington Stoke books are:

Great stories – funny, scary or exciting –
and all by the best writers around!

No hassle – fast reads with no boring bits,
and a story that you can't put down.

Short – the perfect size for a fast, fun
read.

We use our own font and paper to make it
easier for dyslexic people to read our books
too. And we ask readers like you, who want a
no-hassle read, to check every book before
it's published.

That way, we know for sure that every
Barrington Stoke book is a great read for
everyone.

Check out www.barringtonstoke.co.uk for more
info about Barrington Stoke and our books!

Perry's 5
by
Gareth P. Jones

The gang: Perry's 5.
The plan: To steal a maths exam paper.
To try it would be crazy. But if they do it they'll be heroes.
The con is on – but can Perry and his team pull it off?

Desirable
by
Frank Cottrell Boyce

George is a loser. Then he starts using the aftershave that he got for his birthday. Suddenly all the girls are in love with him ... and that includes the teachers! George wanted to be popular. Now he's looking for somewhere to hide ...

You can order these books directly from our website at
www.barringtonstoke.co.uk

Icefall
by
John Townsend

A nose-stud. A snake tattoo.
That's all Barney knows about the people who want him dead.
He doesn't know why they want to kill him.
Or what they'll do next.
All he knows is they'll stop at nothing ...

Hunted
by
Elizabeth Kay

When Tim travels to Africa with his step-brother Martin, he has no idea of the adventure ahead of them.
A dead elephant, gun-shots, ivory poachers.
As the sun goes down, there is no place to hide...
Will they be *hunted?*

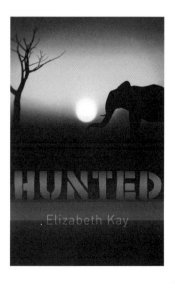

You can order these books directly from our website at
www.barringtonstoke.co.uk